The Boy and the Goats

by Margaret Hillert

Illustrated by Yoshi Miyake

NORWOOD HOUSE PRESS

DEAR CAREGIVER, The *Beginning-to-Read* series is a carefully written collection of classic readers you may remember from your own childhood. Each book features text comprised of common sight words to provide your child ample practice reading the words that appear most frequently in written text. The many additional details in the pictures enhance the story and offer the opportunity for you to help your child expand oral language and develop comprehension.

Begin by reading the story to your child, followed by letting him or her read familiar words and soon your child will be able to read the story independently. At each step of the way, be sure to praise your reader's efforts to build his or her confidence as an independent reader. Discuss the pictures and encourage your child to make connections between the story and his or her own life. At the end of the story, you will find reading activities and a word list that will help your child practice and strengthen beginning reading skills.

Above all, the most important part of the reading experience is to have fun and enjoy it!

Shannon Cannon

Shannon Cannon,
Literacy Consultant

Norwood House Press • P.O. Box 316598 • Chicago, Illinois 60631
For more information about Norwood House Press please visit our website at *www.norwoodhousepress.com* or call 866-565-2900.

LIBRARY OF CONGRESS CATALOGING-IN-PUBLICATION DATA

Hillert, Margaret.
 The boy and the goats / Margaret Hillert; illustrated by Yoshi Miyake. —
Rev. and expanded library ed.
   p. cm. — (Beginning-to-read book)
   Summary: A rabbit, a fox, a wolf, and a bumblebee try to help a little boy
get his stray goats back from the next field. Includes reading activities.
   ISBN-13: 978-1-59953-053-6 (library binding : alk. paper)
   ISBN-10: 1-59953-053-8 (library binding : alk. paper)
   [1. Folklore.] I. Miyake, Yoshi, ill. II. Title. III. Series: Hillert,
Margaret. Beginning to read series. Fairy tales and folklore.
   PZ8.1.H539Bo 2007
   398.24'529735—dc22
   [E]   2006007898

Come, goats.
Come with me.
We will go for a walk and
find something for you to eat.

This is a good spot.
You can eat here.
Eat, eat, eat.

Oh, oh.
Do not do that.
You can not eat that.
Jump out. Jump out.

Oh, no!
Not you, too.
This will not do.
Get out! Get out!

What will I do?
What will I do now?
I want my goats to come
here to me.

What is it, little boy?
What is it?
Can I help you?

My goats will not come out.
What can you do?
How can you help?

I will run at the goats.
Look what I can do.

Oh, no.
That did not work, did it?
That did not work.

Oh, my. Oh, my.
What have we here?
What is it, you two?

We can not make my
goats come out.
Look at that.
The goats will not jump out.

I will help you.
See me run at the goats.

I guess it did not work.
I am no help to you.

My, my.
Look at you three.
How funny you look.
What is it?

My goats eat and eat and
will not come here to me.
What am I to do?

Oh, I will work for you.
I will help.
This is something I am good at.
Go, goats, go.

Oh, my!
The goats did not go out.
What can I do now?

Here. Here.
What is it?
You do not look good.

My goats will not come to me.
No one can help me.
What am I to do?

I can help you.
I can make the goats come out.
Do you want me to help?

You!
You are funny.
How can you make the
goats come out?
You are too little.

You will see.
I am little, but I can do it.
Here I go.

And here come my goats.
You did it!
You did it!
Oh, you are good.

Come, goats.
Come on. Come on.
You are out, and we can go now.

READING REINFORCEMENT

The following activities support the findings of the National Reading Panel that determined the most effective components for reading instruction are: Phonemic Awareness, Phonics, Vocabulary, Fluency, and Text Comprehension.

Phonemic Awareness: The /g/ sound

Oral Blending: Say the beginning sounds listed below and ask your child to say the word formed by adding the /**g**/ sound to the end:

lo + /g/ = log	wa + /g/ = wag	le + /g/ = leg
fla + /g/ = flag	du + /g/ = dug	twi + /g/ = twig
hu + /g/ = hug	mu + /g/ = mug	ba + /g/ = bag
snu + /g/ = snug	fro + /g/ = frog	dra + /g/ = drag

Phonics: The letter Gg

1. Demonstrate how to form the letters **G** and **g** for your child.

2. Have your child practice writing **G** and **g** at least three times each.

3. Ask your child to point to the words in the book that begin with the letter **g**.

4. Write down the following words and ask your child to circle the letter **g** in each word:

garden	grin	gap	go	peg
wiggle	flag	gate	game	plug
jug	piglet	girl	log	large

Vocabulary: Prepositions

1. Explain to your child that some words help us to understand when something happens or where it is. These words are called prepositions.

2. Write the following words on separate pieces of paper:

above	after	before	below	down	far
in	near	out	over	under	up

3. Read each word to your child.

4. Mix up the words.

5. Read each of the following sentences. Say the underlined preposition in the sentence and ask your child to point to the piece of paper that has the preposition. Ask your child to name the object that the preposition is describing.

- The clouds in the sky are <u>above</u> my head. (clouds)
- When we raise the flag, it goes <u>up</u> the pole. (flag)
- I keep a box of toys <u>under</u> my bed. (box of toys)
- We have a library <u>near</u> our house. (library)
- I can play with my friend <u>after</u> my homework is done. (homework)

6. Mix up the words again and work with your child to match the opposite preposition pairs (before/after, up/down, in/out, near/far, above/below etc.).

Fluency: Shared Reading

1. Reread the story to your child at least two more times while your child tracks the print by running a finger under the words as they are read. Ask your child to read the words he or she knows with you.

2. Reread the story taking turns, alternating readers between sentences or pages.

Text Comprehension: Discussion Time

1. Ask your child to retell the sequence of events in the story.

2. To check comprehension, ask your child the following questions:

- Why was the boy sad?
- How did the rabbit try to help the boy?
- Why do you think the goats did not want to come out?
- Who finally helped the boy get the goats to come out?
- Can you describe a time when you needed someone to help you do something?
- What lesson do you think the boy learned?

WORD LIST

The Boy and the Goats uses the 59 words listed below.

This list can be used to practice reading the words that appear in the text. You may wish to write the words on index cards and use them to help your child build automatic word recognition. Regular practice with these words will enhance your child's fluency in reading connected text.

a	get	make	that
am	go	me	the
and	goats	my	this
are	good		three
at	guess	no	to
		not	too
boy	have	now	two
but	help		
	here	oh	walk
can	how	on	want
come		one	we
	I	out	what
did	is		will
do	it	run	with
			work
eat	jump	see	
		something	you
find	little	spot	
for	look		
funny			

ABOUT THE AUTHOR Margaret Hillert has written over 80 books for children who are just learning to read. Her books have been translated into many different languages and over a million children throughout the world have read her books. She first started writing poetry as a child and has continued to write for children and adults throughout her life. A first grade teacher for 34 years, Margaret is now retired from teaching and lives in Michigan where she likes to write, take walks in the morning, and care for her three cats.

Photograph by Glenna Washburn

ABOUT THE ADVISER Shannon Cannon contributed the activities pages that appear in this book. Shannon serves as a literacy consultant and provides staff development to help improve reading instruction. She is a frequent presenter at educational conferences and workshops. Prior to this she worked as an elementary school teacher and as president of a curriculum publishing company.